Calendar Mysteries

September Sneakers

by Ron Roy

illustrated by
John Steven Gurney

A STEPPING STONE BOOK™

Random House 🏠 New York

*This book is dedicated to anyone who
has ever given a child a book.*
—R.R.

To Ruthie and Grace
—J.S.G.

Text copyright © 2013 by Ron Roy
Cover art, map, and interior illustrations copyright © 2013 by John Steven Gurney

All rights reserved. Published in the United States by Random House Children's
Books, a division of Random House, Inc., New York.

Random House and the colophon are registered trademarks and A Stepping Stone
Book and the colophon are trademarks of Random House, Inc.

Visit us on the Web!
ronroy.com
randomhouse.com/kids

Educators and librarians, for a variety of teaching tools, visit us at
RHTeachersLibrarians.com

Library of Congress Cataloging-in-Publication Data
Roy, Ron.
September sneakers / by Ron Roy ; illustrated by John Steven Gurney. — 1st ed.
  p. cm. — (Calendar mysteries) "A Stepping Stone Book."
Summary: Someone has been stealing and leaving behind little green sneakers, so
Bradley, Brian, Nate, and Lucy trail their new teacher, who wears the same shoes in
normal size.
ISBN 978-0-375-86887-0 (trade) — ISBN 978-0-375-96887-7 (lib. bdg.) —
ISBN 978-0-375-89970-6 (ebook)
[1. Mystery and detective stories. 2. Stealing—Fiction. 3. Sneakers—Fiction.
4. Teachers—Fiction. 5. Twins—Fiction. 6. Brothers and sisters—Fiction. 7. Cousins—
Fiction.] I. Gurney, John Steven, ill. II. Title.
PZ7.R8139Sf 2013
[Fic]—dc23
2012009242

Printed in the United States of America

10 9 8 7 6 5 4 3 2 1

Contents

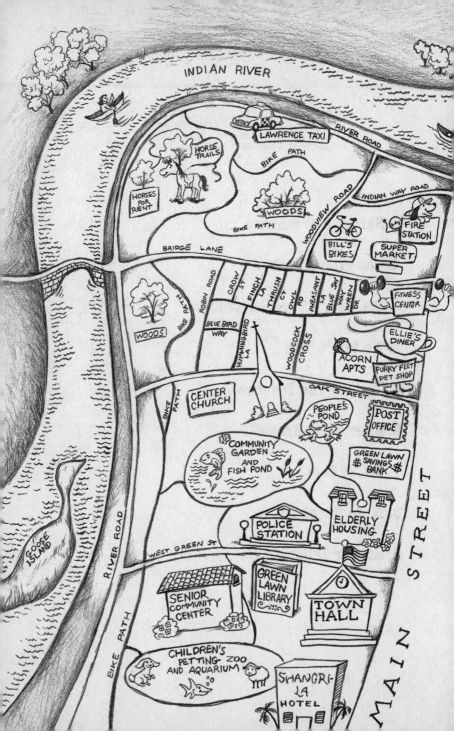

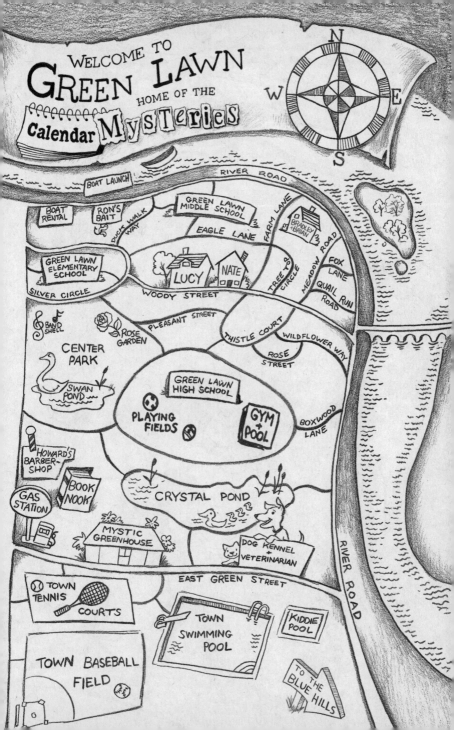

1
Surprise at Sunrise

"Come on, Pal, let's go visit Goldi," Bradley Pinto said to his dog. Pal followed Bradley and his twin brother, Brian, and their friends Nate Hathaway and Lucy Armstrong to the barn. It was the last day of summer vacation!

Bradley was keeping Goldilocks, his first-grade class's pet hamster, over the summer. She lived in an aquarium in the barn. The Pintos' pony, Polly, also lived in the barn.

The leaves on the maple trees near

the barn were just starting to turn red. A September breeze bent the tall grass in the meadow. The kids were wearing T-shirts and jeans.

"I can't believe summer is gone," Lucy said. "But I can't wait to meet our new teacher!" Lucy was staying with her cousin Dink Duncan for a year. Her parents were helping build a school on a reservation in Arizona.

"I wish we could have Mr. Vooray as a teacher again," Nate said. "He tells good jokes!"

Nate was Ruth Rose's little brother. Ruth Rose and Dink were best friends with Josh, the twins' older brother.

"But we're in second grade now," Brian said.

The kids walked into the barn. Pal ran ahead. His long ears almost touched the ground.

"Pal is going to miss Goldi when we

bring her back to school tomorrow," Nate said.

Bradley walked over to the work-bench. Goldi the hamster sat up in her cage and began squeaking. The kids carried the cage outside. Pal followed them.

They set the aquarium on the grass and took off the cover. Pal flopped down on his stomach. Bradley reached in and picked up Goldi. She felt warm in his hands. He put her down next to Pal.

Pal began poking the hamster with his nose. Goldi climbed up Pal's nose and sat on his head.

"We should take pictures!" Brian said. "I'll bet we have the only dog who lets a hamster sit on his head!"

The kids sat on the lawn and watched Goldi walk on Pal's back. When she got to his tail, she turned around and walked back to his head.

Bradley pulled a leaf of lettuce from

his pocket. He set Goldi on the ground and put it in front of her. Goldi started to nibble on the lettuce. Pal nibbled the other end.

"I wonder if Pal knows Goldi is leaving tomorrow," Nate said.

"We should buy Pal a stuffed hamster so he doesn't get lonely," Brian said.

"Pal will know the difference," Bradley said. "Stuffed hamsters don't smell like real hamsters. Pal can smell Goldi a mile away!"

Just then the back door opened. "Lunch is ready!" Bradley and Brian's mom yelled.

The kids put Goldi back in her cage and carried it into the barn. Pal followed them and barked.

"He's saying good-bye," Bradley said.

The next morning Bradley and Brian got up early for school. They were eating breakfast when they heard a knock at the back door. They looked through the glass and saw Nate and Lucy.

"Be right out!" Brian yelled. He slurped the milk from his cereal bowl. Both boys put their bowls and spoons in the sink. They popped their heads into the living room to say good-bye to their parents. Then they grabbed their book bags and raced out the back door.

"Let's go get Goldi," Bradley said. "We can carry the aquarium to school in my old wagon."

All four kids were wearing new shirts and new sneakers. They carried new pencils and lunches in their book bags.

Bradley ran into the barn first. But then he stopped in his tracks. Lucy bumped into him. Nate and Brian peered over their shoulders.

The aquarium was gone.

2
The First Sneaker

"Where's Goldi?" Bradley asked.

"She was right there!" Brian said, pointing to the space on the workbench. "Her food is gone, too!"

"What's this?" Lucy asked. She picked up a tiny sneaker from the workbench. The three-inch-long sneaker was bright green. There was an orange lightning bolt on one side. The sneaker was attached to a chain with a key ring on the end.

Bradley looked around the barn.

Maybe Josh had moved the aquarium. He saw a lawn mower, two old tires, and a few rakes and shovels. He did not see a golden hamster with shiny black eyes.

"It's pet-nappers!" Nate cried.

"Search the barn!" Brian yelled. They all scattered, peeking in every dark corner.

Bradley thought of Polly. He sprinted to the pony's stall. She was there, looking at him with big brown eyes. "At least they didn't take you," he said.

Suddenly Pal let out a howl. He sniffed the barn floor and raced out into the yard. A minute later he came back. He sat under the workbench and whimpered.

"Pal smells the hamster stealer!" Nate said.

"Maybe whoever took the aquarium left this little sneaker here," Lucy said.

"Dibs on the sneaker!" Brian said.

He snatched the sneaker and attached it to his book bag.

"The kids at school are going to hate me!" Bradley said. "I was supposed to take care of Goldi!"

"It's not your fault, bro," his twin said. "The crook must have come during the night."

The kids walked to school. Bradley felt an ache in his stomach. He had been so happy about the first day of school. Now he felt rotten.

They were all looking up at the leaves, which were starting to change to yellow and red. The sun behind them made their shadows long.

When they got close to the school building, Bradley noticed something. A pair of green sneakers was hanging from a tree branch. They were normal size, like an adult would wear.

Both sneakers had an orange lightning bolt.

"Look," Bradley said, pointing up at the sneakers.

Brian grabbed the little sneaker hanging on his book bag. He held it up. "They're exactly like this one!" he said.

"Who put them there?" Nate said. "They look brand-new!"

The kids heard a bell and ran toward the school. Mr. Dillon, the principal, stood on the front steps. He shook hands with each of them.

"Welcome back!" he said. "You're second graders now, right?"

"Yes, sir," the kids said.

"Wonderful! Your new teacher is Ms. Tery," Mr. Dillon said. "I know you'll enjoy getting to know her. Now scoot along and have a great first day!"

Bradley had seen Ms. Tery around the school last year. He hoped she was as nice as Mr. Vooray.

The kids hurried into the building. It

was noisy. Kids were trying to find their rooms. A few moms and dads stood around looking worried. One little girl was crying as her mother tried to take her into a classroom. Some older boys were yelling at each other.

Bradley, Brian, Nate, and Lucy headed for the second-grade classroom. They passed Mr. Vooray's room.

"You guys go ahead," Bradley said to the other kids. "I've got to tell Mr. Vooray about Goldi."

"Not alone, you don't," Lucy said. "We're all going to tell him."

Lucy pushed open the door to Mr. Vooray's room. Most of the seats were filled with first graders. They all stared at the four second graders.

Mr. Vooray smiled when he saw Bradley, Brian, Nate, and Lucy. "Hello there!" he said. "Your new room is next door, remember?"

"We know," Bradley said. "But we have something to tell you."

"Sure," Mr. Vooray said. He leaned against his desk. "I'm all ears."

Mr. Vooray picked up a key ring from the desktop and attached it to his belt loop.

Bradley stared. Dangling from the ring was a miniature green sneaker with an orange lightning bolt.

3

Ms. Tery's Favorite Colors

Bradley didn't know what to say. Why did Mr. Vooray have a little green sneaker?

"Tell him," Nate said, giving Bradley a poke in the back.

"Um, when we went to get Goldi this morning, she was gone," Bradley said.

Mr. Vooray looked confused. "Goldi is gone?" he asked. "Gone where?"

"We don't know!" Bradley said. "We kept her aquarium in our barn all summer long. When we went to get her this morning, it wasn't there!"

Mr. Vooray's face went from happy to sad. "Who would steal a little hamster?" he asked.

"And look what the crooks left!" Brian said. He showed Mr. Vooray the green sneaker clipped to his book bag.

Mr. Vooray stared at the sneaker. He unclipped his key ring and showed the kids his little green sneaker. "I found this on my back porch this morning," he said.

"Wow!" Lucy said. "It's exactly like ours!"

Bradley stared and blinked. "Um, did . . . did they take anything?"

"Darn right they did!" Mr. Vooray said. "My favorite tennis racket was on the porch, and now it isn't!"

"Oh gosh, there's a maniac in Green Lawn!" Nate howled.

Mr. Vooray shook his head. "It's

probably someone pulling a joke," he said. "Not a very nice one."

"We really want Goldi back!" Brian said. "We loved playing with her in your class last year."

"Yeah, my new first graders will be disappointed, too," Mr. Vooray said. "Thanks for telling me."

A loud bell went off. The four kids walked to the next room. A little sign on the door said WELCOME TO SECOND GRADE.

Bradley reached for the doorknob. But the door was yanked open before his fingers touched it.

"Perfect timing!" a voice said from near the ceiling.

Standing in front of the kids was the tallest woman Bradley had ever seen. She looked like a basketball player on TV. She wore a green sweatshirt that said BOSTON CELTICS on the front. Her skirt was long and orange, almost touching

the floor. Her red hair hung in a thick braid down her back. She had blue eyes that stared down at the kids.

The giant woman smiled. "Come on in. I don't bite," she said.

The rest of the second graders in the class laughed.

Bradley recognized a lot of the kids from first grade last year.

"I'm Ms. Tery. In case you're wondering why I'm so tall, it's because I eat all my vegetables!" she said. "Now find a place to park, please."

The four kids all found seats, but not next to each other.

"You know who I am," Ms. Tery said to the class, "but I don't know you. When I point to you, stand up and tell us your name. Then tell us something interesting about yourself."

She pointed to Julie, in the front row.

Julie hopped up. "I'm Juliette

Jackson, but my friends call me Julie. This summer I learned how to swim. Almost!"

"Can I go next?" Bobby Arnold asked.

Ms. Tery smiled again. "Of course."

Bobby stood up. "I'm Bobby Arnold," he said. "My basketball got stolen last night! We live on Blue Jay Way. I left my ball in the front yard. It was gone this morning. I found this right where I left the ball." He held up a little green sneaker.

"Me too!" a kid named Zack said. He held up a tiny green sneaker. "Somebody took my bathing suit right off the clothesline!"

Bradley stared at Zack's and Bobby's little green sneakers. They were just like the one they'd found in their barn.

"Us too!" Brian yelled. He waved his little green sneaker at the class. "Someone stole our hamster. Well, really

Mr. Vooray's hamster. We were keeping her over the summer. They left us a green sneaker, too!"

"Someone stole Mr. Vooray's hamster?" Ms. Tery almost yelled. "That's just awful!"

Caitlyn waved her hand. "My grandma called me last night," she said. "I gave her a flower for her birthday and she kept it on her front porch. When she went to water it this morning, it was gone!"

"Goodness!" Ms. Tery said. "Did your grammy find a little sneaker?"

"Yes!" Caitlyn said. She pointed at Brian's. "Like that!"

"It seems we have a sneaker mystery in Green Lawn," Ms. Tery said. She raised her skirt a few inches and pointed down at her feet.

Everyone in the class looked at her shoes.

Only they weren't just any school-teacher shoes.

They were giant green sneakers.

And they had orange lightning bolts on the sides.

4
We Don't Bite

Bradley's eyes got wide. Was he seeing things?

"But why are your sneakers like these little ones?" Bobby asked Ms. Tery.

"I don't know," the teacher said. "It's very curious!"

"Um, there are other green sneakers, too," Bradley said. He told Ms. Tery and the class about the ones they'd seen hanging from the tree branch. "Only those were regular size."

"Well, I don't know what's going

on," Ms. Tery said. "But I think someone is having some fun with us."

"But what about the stuff they took?" Caitlyn asked.

"And Mr. Vooray's hamster?" Brian added. "That's not funny!"

"I wish I had an answer," Ms. Tery said. "We'll just have to wait and see what happens next with the Green Lawn sneaker sneak!"

Ms. Tery walked to the chalkboard. "Take out your pencils, please." Then she wrote:

CLASS RULES:
WE ARE POLITE.
WE DON'T FIGHT.
WE DON'T BITE.

"It rhymes!" Nate said. "Cool!"

"Who likes rhyming?" Ms. Tery asked.

Most of the kids raised their hands.

"Good! I do, too," she said. "We're going to write every morning. Today, try to write a rhyming poem. It can be about anything, even our sneaker mystery."

She passed out paper. Kids opened their desks and book bags and pencil boxes.

"Be as quiet as mice," Ms. Tery whispered.

The class hunched over their desks and began writing.

Bradley had never written a poem before. He stared at the boy in front of him. All he could think of was Goldi being stolen.

"How are you doing, second-grade writers?" Ms. Tery suddenly asked. She swooped down the aisles like a pterodactyl.

Bradley grabbed his pencil and wrote the first thing that popped into his head:

once i met a talking worm.
His name was sherm.

Ms. Tery's shadow fell on Bradley's paper. "That's a nice beginning," she said. "Capital *O* and capital *I*, please."

"Thank you, Ms. Tery," Bradley mumbled. He fixed the *O* and the *I*.

After a while, Ms. Tery had some of the kids read their poems.

Then they practiced adding and subtracting.

At noon, they all went to the school cafeteria for lunch. It was pretty noisy, so everyone ate fast, then went outside for recess. Bradley, Brian, Nate, and Lucy sat under a tree.

Across the playground, they saw Ms. Tery talking with a few other teachers. She was at least a foot taller than they were.

Lucy sipped her milk. "What if Ms. Tery is the person who's taking stuff and leaving the tiny sneakers?" she asked. "There has to be a reason why the little sneakers look exactly like hers."

"And the ones in the tree," Nate said.

"None of it makes sense," Bradley said. "I just want Goldi back!"

"So what do we do?" Brian asked.

"We should follow Ms. Tery home," Bradley whispered. "If she's stealing stuff, maybe we'll catch her in the act!"

5
Trailing the Teacher

A soccer ball shot past Bradley. When he grabbed the ball, he saw some high school kids walking by the school. The tallest kid had another boy on his shoulders. Two of the others were tossing a basketball back and forth. They were pretty big, so Bradley figured they were seniors.

The school bell sounded, and Bradley bounded back to the other kids. He carried the soccer ball and handed it to Ms. Tery.

"Thank you, Brian," Ms. Tery said.

"I'm Bradley," Bradley said.

She grinned. "Who says?"

"I have bigger freckles than my brother," Bradley said.

Ms. Tery made the kids wash their hands. Then she marched them to the school library. "Walk single file, like little ducks," she said. "And no quacking!"

Bradley picked a book called *Charlotte's Web*. The cover showed a big spider hanging from its web and a girl with a pig in her arms.

When it was almost time to go home, Ms. Tery told the kids they could read quietly for a few minutes. She walked around the room, checking out everyone's books.

At Bradley's desk she stopped. "I love that book," she said. "But I really don't like spiders!" Ms. Tery rubbed her arms. "Spiders give me goose bumps!"

A few minutes later the bell rang.

"Class dismissed!" Ms. Tery called out. "See you tomorrow!"

The kids jumped out of their seats. Bradley nodded good-bye to Ms. Tery. He had a lump in his throat. Were they really going to spy on their teacher?

Outside, Bradley, Brian, Nate, and Lucy hid behind some bushes on the side of the school. Ms. Tery would have to walk right past them.

"What if she doesn't walk home?" Lucy asked. "What if she has a car?"

"I never thought of that," Bradley said.

They sat and waited. They heard teachers saying good-bye. They heard car doors slam and engines start.

Bradley heard a bird call and looked up into the nearest tree. It was the same tree where the sneakers had been hanging. Only now they were gone.

Suddenly his brother grabbed his arm. "She's coming!" Brian whispered.

Ms. Tery loped past them, heading for Main Street. She carried a shopping bag with a picture of a kangaroo on the side.

"She's walking!" Bradley whispered.

"I'll bet she carries the stuff she steals in that bag!" Nate said.

"Or maybe it's filled with tiny sneakers," Brian offered.

6
Brian Sees Broccoli

The kids watched Ms. Tery cross Main Street.

"She's headed for Bridge Lane," Nate remarked.

"Let's go before we lose her!" Brian said.

"We can't lose her," Nate sniggered. "She's too tall to lose."

"She's going into the supermarket!" Lucy said.

Ms. Tery disappeared inside the store. The kids waited for a WALK signal, then hurried across Main Street.

"I'll go in to see what she's doing," Brian said. "The rest of you stay out here."

Brian slipped through the supermarket door.

"I wonder if Ms. Tery plans to steal something from the store," Bradley said, "and leave a sneaker behind."

"How cool would it be to have a teacher who goes to jail for shoplifting!" Nate said. "Maybe we'd get a vacation!"

Two minutes later Brian came running through the door.

"Did she see you?" Bradley asked.

Brian shook his head. "Nope. She's in the checkout line," he said. "And guess what she bought?"

"Candy?" Nate guessed.

"Nope," Brian said.

"Hamster food?" Lucy offered.

"Nope."

"Brian, tell us right now!" Bradley said.

"She got a bunch of carrots and some broccoli!" Brian said, his eyes all excited.

The others just looked at him.

"Don't you get it?" Brian said. "She bought orange and green stuff, like all the sneakers!"

"Like her orange skirt and green shirt," Lucy added.

"And look what I found!" Brian whipped a paper from his pocket. He showed it to the others. The printing on the paper said:

SWEET FEET COMING SOON!!!!!

Below the words was a picture of green-and-orange sneakers.

"There was a pile of these flyers inside the door," Brian said.

"What does *sweet feet* mean?" Nate asked.

No one had an answer.

"Yikes, she's coming out!" Nate

hissed. The kids raced behind a row of shopping carts.

Ms. Tery strolled outside and took a right, heading up Bridge Lane. Her shopping bag was fat. Bradley wondered what was in there besides carrots and broccoli. Bobby Arnold's basketball? Mr. Vooray's tennis racket? A hamster named Goldi?

The kids ran behind Bill's Bikes. They

watched Ms. Tery walk past Pheasant Lane and Owl Road. She turned left onto Thrush Court.

The four kids crept from behind the bike shop. They darted toward some hedges on the corner of Bridge Lane and Thrush Court. Now they had a perfect view of their teacher marching up the street.

Ms. Tery turned in at a small yellow

house. She walked up the steps, unlocked the front door, and disappeared inside.

"Now what?" Nate asked. "Want to peek in her windows?"

"No, that would be trespassing," Bradley said. "Let's just walk past her house. If she sees us, we can always say we're going to visit someone."

The kids ambled past the yellow house, looking straight ahead. Bradley stole a peek into the yard. He saw some bushes. He saw a garage with a basketball hoop nailed over the door.

"Look," Nate whispered. He jerked his head toward the front porch. They all saw a basketball on a small bench by the door.

"I wonder if that's Bobby Arnold's," Brian said.

"Don't stop and gawk!" Bradley said. "Let's go back!"

The kids turned around and walked

away. They stopped under a giant tree that grew on the corner of Thrush Court and Bridge Lane. The thick limbs spread all the way to the other side of Bridge Lane.

"If we climbed this tree, we could see right into Ms. Tery's backyard," Brian said.

The others gazed up into the tree.

"Oh no!" Bradley yelled. "There's another one!"

Hanging from a limb ten feet over their heads was a pair of sneakers.

"Green-and-orange sneakers," Nate said. "Looks like the sneaker maniac is following us!"

7
Sweet Feet

"They look just like the ones we saw hanging near the school," Brian said.

"I think they're the same ones," Bradley said. "That other pair is gone. I noticed they were missing after school."

The four kids gazed up at the pair hanging above them. "And you think that's them up there?" Nate asked.

Bradley nodded. "I saw some high school kids near the tree," he said. "They might have taken them down and brought them over here."

"But why?" Brian asked. "This is crazy!"

"I'm going up to get them," Lucy said. She dropped her book bag on the ground and began climbing the tall tree.

"What for?" asked Nate.

Lucy stopped climbing. "Maybe whoever left these sneakers is the same person who put the little one in the barn," she said. "And that person stole Goldi." Lucy pointed up. "These sneakers might be clues!"

Lucy climbed until she came to the limb holding the sneakers. But the limb was too thin for her to go any farther. "I need a long stick," Lucy called down.

The three boys scurried around in the bushes under the tree.

"I got one!" Bradley yelled. He held up a dead branch. "Is this okay?"

"Perfect," Lucy said. "Can you hand it to me?"

"I think so," Bradley said.

"We'll give you a boost," his brother said.

Brian and Nate put their hands together and linked their fingers. This made a step for Bradley's foot. With one hand on his brother's head, Bradley held the branch up to Lucy.

"Got it!" Lucy said. She used the stick to knock the sneakers to the ground.

Lucy scurried down, and Nate plucked a leaf out of her hair.

"Cool climbing, Lucy," he said.

Bradley took a whiff inside one of the sneakers. "They smell new," he said. "Look how white the laces are. I don't think they've even been worn."

"Why would anyone toss a pair of cool new sneakers up into a tree?" asked Nate.

The kids studied the sneakers. They were bright green, with a lightning bolt

on the side. Inside, a label said SWEET
FEET.

"Like the flyer I found in the
supermarket!" Brian said. He held up
the small sneaker they'd found in the
barn. "They're the same, only this little
one doesn't say *sweet feet* inside."

"This is getting weirder and weirder,"
Bradley said.

"Let's head home," Brian said. "My
tummy needs a snack."

They decided to walk down Owl
Road. Nate had the SWEET FEET sneakers
hanging around his neck. Bradley was
studying the flyer, trying to make sense
of it.

Suddenly a voice rang out. "Hey, you
kids!"

A man with gray hair walked over to
them. He was holding a leaf rake.

"You kids live around here?" the man
asked.

"No, we live on the other side of

Main Street," Brian answered.

The man looked suspicious. "What're you doing over here?" he asked.

"We were looking for our teacher," Nate piped up. "Ms. Tery? She lives on Thrush Court."

Finally the man smiled. "Okay, but there's been some stealing going on, and I just wondered."

"What kind of stealing?" Bradley asked.

"Someone took my front doormat," the man said. He pointed to his porch. "It was there last night, and gone this morning. Who'd want an old doormat?"

"Sir, did you find a little green sneaker like this?" Brian asked. He held up the one clipped to his book bag.

"I'll be danged!" the man said. "I found one like that on the porch. Gave it to my grandson."

"It's been happening all over town," Bradley said. He told the man about the kids in school who'd lost stuff. "They took our hamster!"

"My pal Hector lost his garden hose!" the man said. "He lives on Pheasant Lane. I'll ask him if he got one of those sneaker things."

The man shook his head and went back to his raking. The kids waved, then kept walking down Owl Road. "Something very weird is going on in this town," Bradley muttered. "And I intend to find out what!"

Five minutes later the kids piled into the kitchen at Bradley and Brian's house. They found a note and a plate of cookies on the table.

The note said:

Out shopping.
Will be back soon.
Play with Pal!

—Mom

"Cool!" Brian said, grabbing the plate. "Hey, Pal, come and get a cookie!"

Pal came loping into the kitchen with his leash in his mouth. The kids took him out into the yard. Bradley and Brian's older brother, Josh, was sitting at the picnic table. Josh was a freshman in high school this year. He was drawing in a notebook. He slammed it shut when he saw the kids coming.

"Hey," Josh said. "What's going on?" He grabbed a cookie.

"Josh, Goldi got stolen last night!" Brian said.

"No way!" Josh said. "Cute little Goldi? Are you sure she didn't just run away?"

"Not unless she took her aquarium with her," Bradley said.

The kids all explained about the green sneaker mystery. Brian showed Josh the little sneaker, and Nate showed him the big ones.

"Where'd you get these?" Josh asked. He took the sneakers from Nate.

"They were hanging in a tree over on Bridge Lane," Bradley said. "Lucy climbed up and got them."

"Could they be a clue?" Lucy asked. "The little ones look just like these bigger ones."

"I don't know about a clue," Josh said. "But I saw one of the seniors wearing a pair exactly like these in school today."

8
More Sneakers

"You did?" Bradley cried. "Who?"

Josh handed the sneakers to Bradley. "A kid named Will. He plays basketball, and he's in the Junior Inventors club I joined."

Bradley's mind was going a hundred miles an hour. Did this Will kid steal Goldi? Was he leaving little sneakers all over town?

"What's the Junior Inventors club?" Nate asked.

"Just a bunch of kids who like

inventing things," Josh said. He waved his notebook and grinned. "Someday this invention is going to change the world!"

Josh headed for the barn. Nate, Brian, and Lucy sat at the picnic table with the cookies between them. Bradley stood next to the table with the green sneakers in his hand.

Bradley felt a tug. Pal yanked the sneakers out of his hand and dropped them on the ground. His big, wet nose traveled all over the sneakers, inside and out. Then he threw his head back and let out a howl.

Pal flopped down on his belly and tossed one of the sneakers into the air. It landed on his head. Pal whimpered and looked at the kids with big brown eyes.

"He used to look just like that when he was playing with Goldi," Lucy said. "He must miss her."

When he heard *Goldi,* Pal barked.

Then he stuck his snout inside one of the sneakers.

Bradley thought about Pal's sense of smell. He dropped down and clipped the leash on to Pal's collar. "Come on, Pal, let's go to the high school!" he said.

"Why do you want to go there?" Nate asked.

"To find this Will kid Josh mentioned," Bradley said. "He has sneakers like these. If we can find Will, I'll bet we can find out everything else!"

They headed down Farm Lane. Nate was carrying the sneakers, looped around his neck. They cut through a field to get to the high school.

The outdoor basketball court was next to the gym. Three tall kids were shooting hoops. None of them was wearing green-and-orange sneakers. The four kids and Pal walked over to the players.

Bradley took the sneakers from Nate. When one of the big kids looked at him, Bradley held them up. "Do you know who these belong to?" he asked.

All three players walked over. "No, but I've seen a few guys wearing sneakers just like them," one of the boys said. "They're way cool!"

"A few guys?" Brian asked. "Like who?"

"Will Taylor and Buddy Plotsky," the tallest boy said. "And I think Hunter Tery has a pair."

"Hunter Tery?" Bradley asked. "Our teacher is Ms. Tery."

The tall boy grinned. "Yup. Hunter's her kid. Those guys hang out together all the time."

The three boys continued their game. Bradley, Brian, Nate, and Lucy looked at each other. Finally they walked over to a bench and sat.

"Ms. Tery has a kid who owns sneakers like these?" Nate asked.

"I guess a bunch of his friends do, too," Bradley said.

"So how do we know which one owns these?" Nate asked.

Brian pulled out the flyer he'd taken from the supermarket. "And what's up with this?" he asked. He read from the flyer: " 'Sweet feet coming soon!!!!!' "

"Maybe *feet* means sneakers," Nate suggested. "A lot of sneakers have been showing up around here!"

"You're right, Nate," Bradley said. "I wonder if there's a pattern to where the little sneakers have been found. That man on Owl Road found one on his porch. And his friend on Pheasant Lane found one."

"And Bobby Arnold, who lives on Blue Jay Way, got one," Nate said.

"Zack lives on Wren Drive," Brian

said. "He found a little sneaker, too."

"And Mr. Vooray did," Lucy added. "Where does he live?"

"On Eagle Lane," Brian said. "Not too far from our house."

Bradley jumped up. "All those places are pretty near Thrush Court," he said. "Where Ms. Tery lives with her son, Hunter. And Hunter owns green-and-orange sneakers, too!"

"Sneakers that Pal thinks smell like Goldi!" Lucy said.

Bradley grinned. "I think we need to go visit Ms. Tery," he said.

9
Hunter Talks

The kids trekked up Bridge Lane. Pal tugged on his leash, as if he knew exactly where he was going. They stopped in front of the little yellow house on Thrush Court, then walked up the driveway to the garage. The basketball was lying under the hoop. Pal began whimpering and tugging Bradley toward the garage.

Suddenly they heard laughter from inside the garage. Pal began barking and yanked the leash from Bradley's hand. He raced to the garage, barking like crazy.

"Pal, stop!" Bradley yelled. He grabbed the leash and pulled his dog away from the door.

Two things happened at once: A skinny, barefooted teenager opened the garage door. And Ms. Tery came running out of the house. Anyone could tell she was the teenager's mother. Both were tall with big feet and red hair.

The teenager stepped out onto the driveway. He shut the garage door behind him. Bradley noticed a sign on the door. It said DANGER—SPIDERS INSIDE. NO MOMS ALLOWED!

"Well, hello there," Ms. Tery said to Bradley, Brian, Nate, and Lucy. "What brings you to my humble home?"

"Hi, Ms. Tery," Bradley said. "We came to talk to your son."

"I don't even know these kids, Mom," the tall boy said.

Nate held up the sneakers. "Do you know these?" he asked.

Hunter Tery blushed as red as his hair.

"Those look just like mine!" Ms. Tery said. "Are they yours, Hunter?"

"Yeah, they're mine," Hunter said. He took the sneakers and slipped them onto his feet.

Pal was barking wildly at the garage door.

"Is this your pooch?" Ms. Tery asked Bradley. "What does he want in our garage?"

"I'm not sure, but I think our hamster might be in there," Brian said. "Pal can smell her, right, boy?"

This made Pal bark even louder.

"Do you mean the hamster that got stolen?" Ms. Tery asked. "Hunter, do you know anything about a hamster?"

Hunter looked at his feet. "Um, yeah, I guess," he said.

"You guess?" his mother said. "Well, I guess I need an explanation."

Hunter sighed. Then he pulled open the garage door. "Come on in," he said.

"No way!" his mother said. "You know how I feel about spiders!"

"There aren't any spiders, Mom," Hunter said. "The sign was to keep you out."

Ms. Tery walked into the garage. The four kids followed her inside. Hunter came last. He left the door open.

Two other teenagers were sitting at a workbench. "Hi, Ms. Tery," they both mumbled.

"Hello, Will. Hello, Buddy," Ms. Tery said. "What're you fellas working on?"

A laptop computer sat on the workbench. Each boy had a notebook in front of him.

"It's our invention project," Hunter told his mother.

"Oh, yes, the one that's a big secret," she said. "And does this project involve stealing a hamster?"

Bradley noticed that Will and Buddy were wearing green-and-orange sneakers, like Hunter's.

"Not exactly, Mom," Hunter said. He walked to the back of the garage. There was a sheet covering a lumpy mound on the floor. Hunter pulled the sheet off. Bradley saw the aquarium, a tennis racket, and a bunch of other stuff. Hunter came back with Goldi in his hands.

"Goldi!" the four younger kids cried.
Pal nearly went crazy barking.

Hunter handed the hamster to Brian,
who put him on the floor in front of
Pal. Pal got flat on the floor, and Goldi
climbed up on his nose. "All the other
stuff we took is back there," Hunter said.

Ms. Tery gave her son a long look.

"Have a seat and explain, please," she said.

Hunter folded his lanky body onto the bench next to Will and Buddy. "We belong to the Junior Inventors club at school," he said. "We decided to invent a new kind of sneaker."

Will and Buddy held up their feet to show off theirs.

Hunter pointed to his mother's sneakers. "I got the green-and-orange idea from yours, Mom," he said. "Our plan was to invent sneakers that didn't smell, even after you wore them a lot. We call them Sweet Feet. Will is real good in science, and he came up with this formula for the soles. His dad helped us find a company that agreed to make them. But first they wanted us to try them out, so they sent a few sample pairs."

Hunter pointed down at his feet. "We

were supposed to wear them to see if the formula worked," he went on. "But I decided to hang my pair around town to get people curious. I hung them in trees where people would see them and want to buy them."

"What about the little ones?" Brian asked.

"The company sent us a bunch," he said. "We decided to leave them at people's houses, to get them interested."

"But why take the hamster?" his mother asked. "And those other things?"

"That was Buddy's big idea," Hunter said. "But we were going to give it all back, honest! Buddy figured people would notice the miniature sneakers even more if we took something and left a little sample sneaker in the same spot."

"It worked," Bradley said. "We noticed!"

No one said anything for a long

minute. Bradley snuck a look at Ms. Tery. She was staring at Hunter. The kids watched Goldi walk along Pal's back. Pal was the only one in the garage with a happy look on his face.

"Okay, Hunter, while I'm trying to figure out your punishment, you can apologize to these kids," Ms. Tery said. "Then you three can return everything you took and apologize to those other people. Okay?"

"I'm real sorry," Hunter told Bradley, Brian, Nate, and Lucy. "We were just trying to promote our sneakers. We didn't mean to upset anybody."

"Yeah, I'm sorry, too," Buddy said. "I guess it was a stupid idea to take things."

"Me too," Will said. "I'll get the company to send you kids some Sweet Feet sneakers, okay?"

"Awesome!" Nate yelled.

"Um, Pal should get sneakers, too,"

Bradley said, patting his dog's head. "Without his nose, we wouldn't have been able to find Goldi."

Hunter opened a notebook and started writing. "Okay, four pairs of sneakers for four second graders."

Then he wrote something else. "And two more pairs for a dog named Pal!"

Pal barked.

Turn the page for a sneak peek at
Bradley, Brian, Nate, and Lucy's
next exciting mystery:

Available now!

"How do I look?" Bradley asked. He was wearing a cardboard box. His head stuck out through a hole in the top, and his feet came out the bottom. There were holes in the sides for his arms.

Bradley had pasted pictures of Presidents George Washington, Abraham Lincoln, Theodore Roosevelt, and Thomas Jefferson on the four sides.

"You look like a box of cereal," Nate said.

Bradley grinned. "I'm Mount Rushmore," he said.

It was Halloween, and the kids were getting dressed at Nate's house. They were going to the Shangri-la Hotel. For Halloween, the building had been changed into a haunted house. All the kids they knew were planning to be there.

Bradley's twin brother, Brian, was dressed as an astronaut. A clear plastic salad bowl covered his red hair. He pretended to breathe through a vacuum-cleaner hose taped to the bowl. His shirt and pants were covered with tinfoil.

Lucy was dressed as Sacagawea. She wore a fake-leather dress and moccasins and had her hair in a braid.

Nate had wound strips of rags around his face and body. "Guess what I am!" he said.

"Raggedy Andy?" Brian joked.

"No, I'm a mummy," Nate said.

The kids left Nate's house and walked to Main Street. The sun was down, but it was not quite dark. They waited at the traffic light in front of Howard's Barbershop.

"Dink told me there's an ogre's cave inside the hotel," Lucy said. "The ogre is guarding a basket of candy. If we steal candy without getting caught, we get a prize!"

When the sign said walk, they crossed Main Street and walked to the Shangri-la Hotel. They stood behind some bushes and looked at the hotel.

"It does look haunted," Lucy said. Bats, witch faces, and skeletons peered out the windows. Thick cobwebs hung from the front door. Spooky music came through the open windows.

A tall green ogre stood at the door. The monster had a lumpy green face and a fat belly. He held a club in his chubby fingers.

If you like Calendar Mysteries, you might want to read A to Z Mysteries!

Help Dink, Josh, and Ruth Rose . . .

Track down all these books

A to Z Mysteries®
by Ron Roy

Calendar Mysteries
by Ron Roy

Capital Mysteries
by Ron Roy

Ballpark Mysteries
by David A. Kelly

The Case of the Elevator Duck
by Polly Berrien Berends

Ghost Horse
by George Edward Stanley

How many of KC and Marshall's adventures have you read?

Capital Mysteries